Jumping

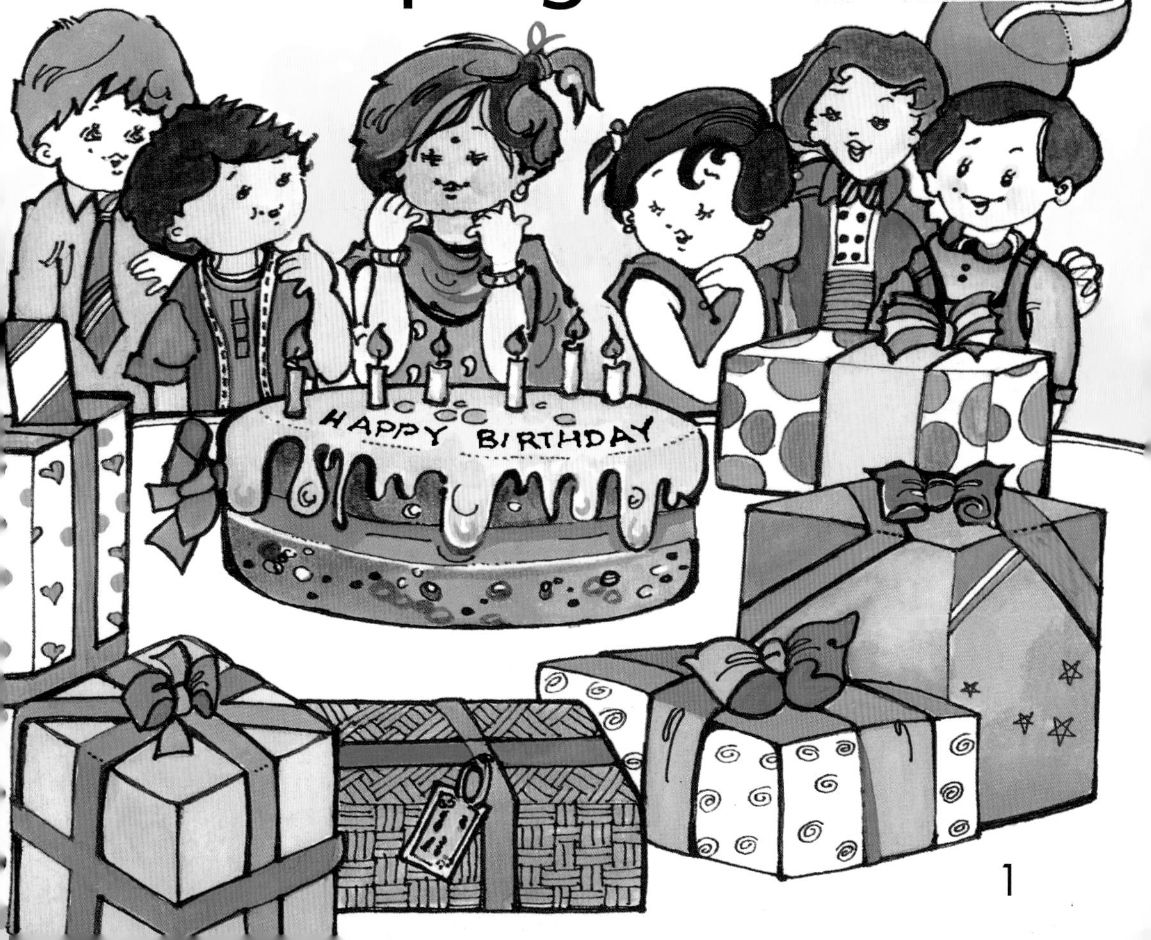

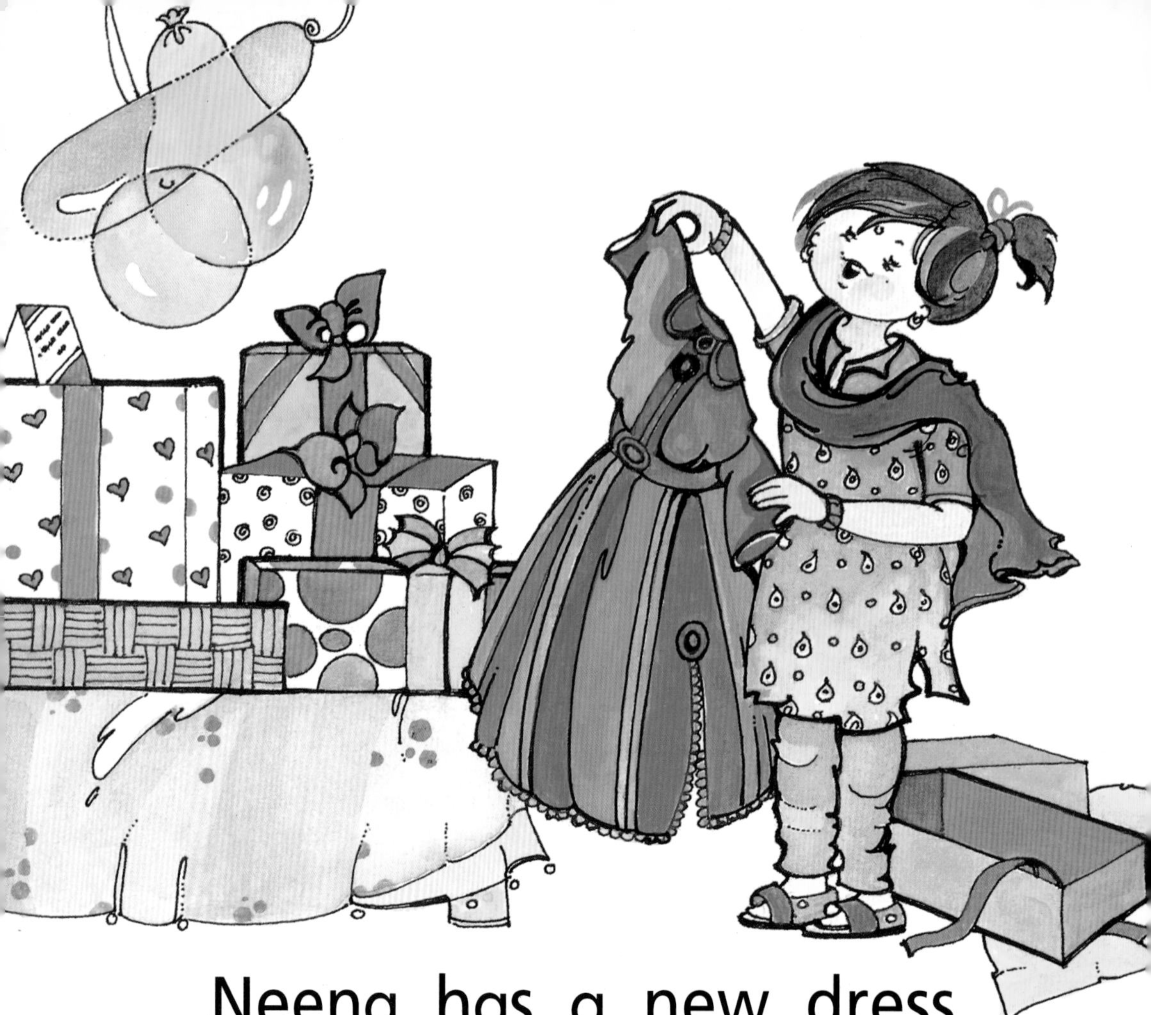

Neena has a new dress.

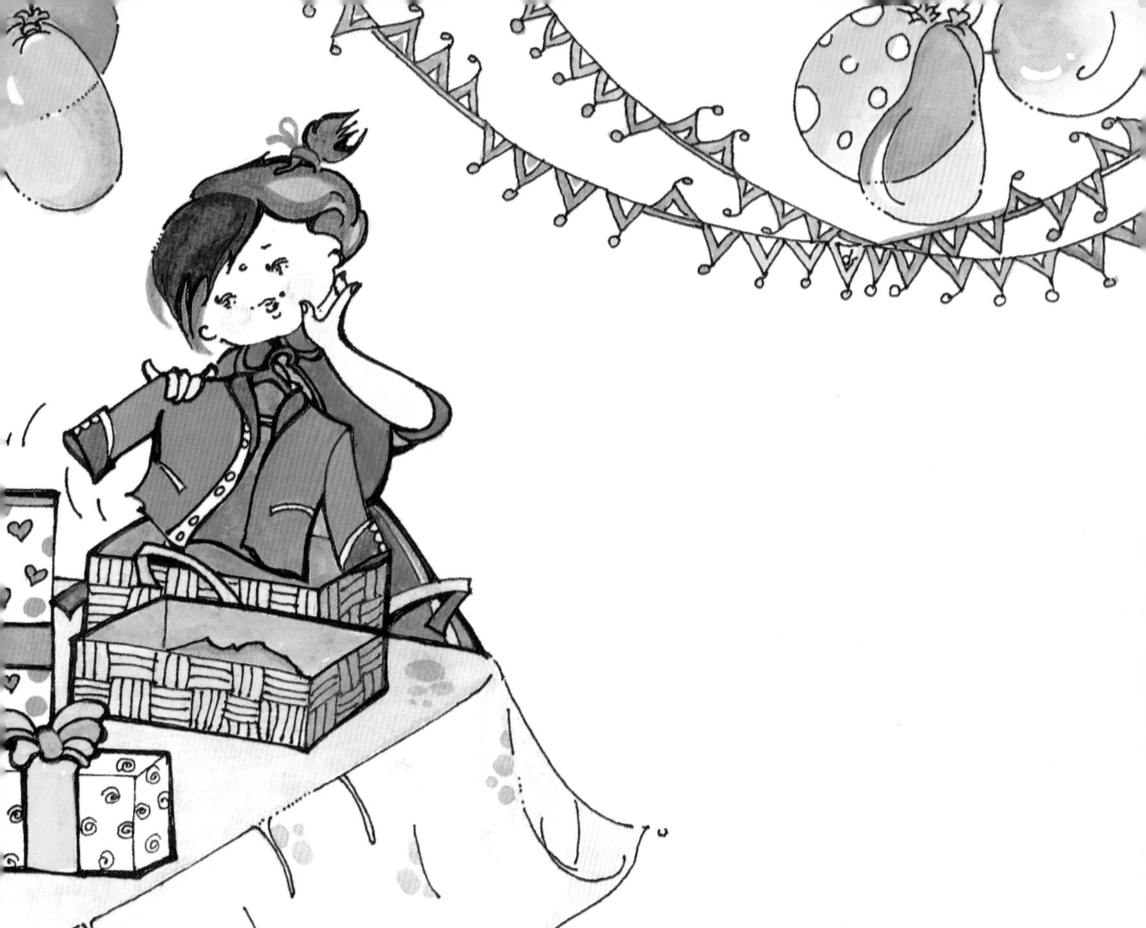

Neena has a new jacket.

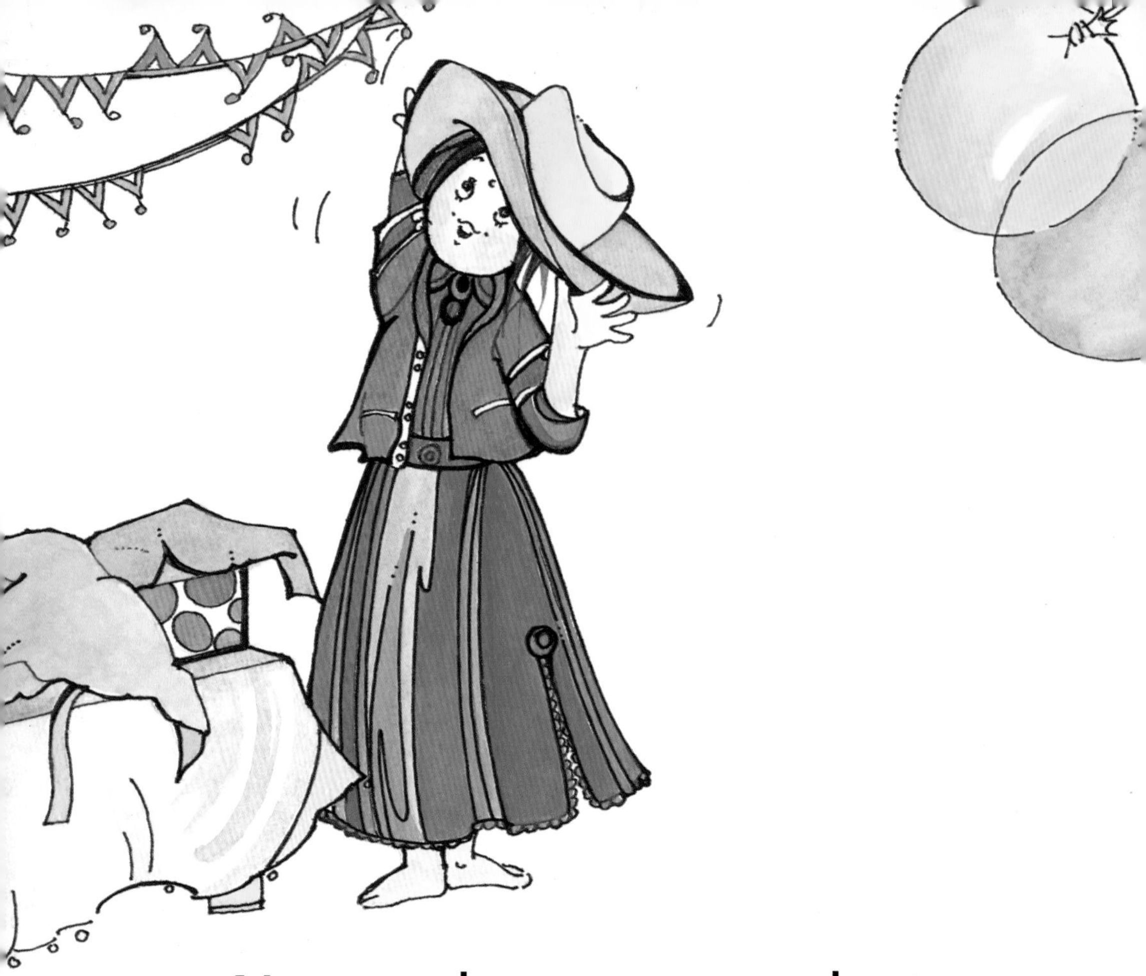

Neena has a new hat.

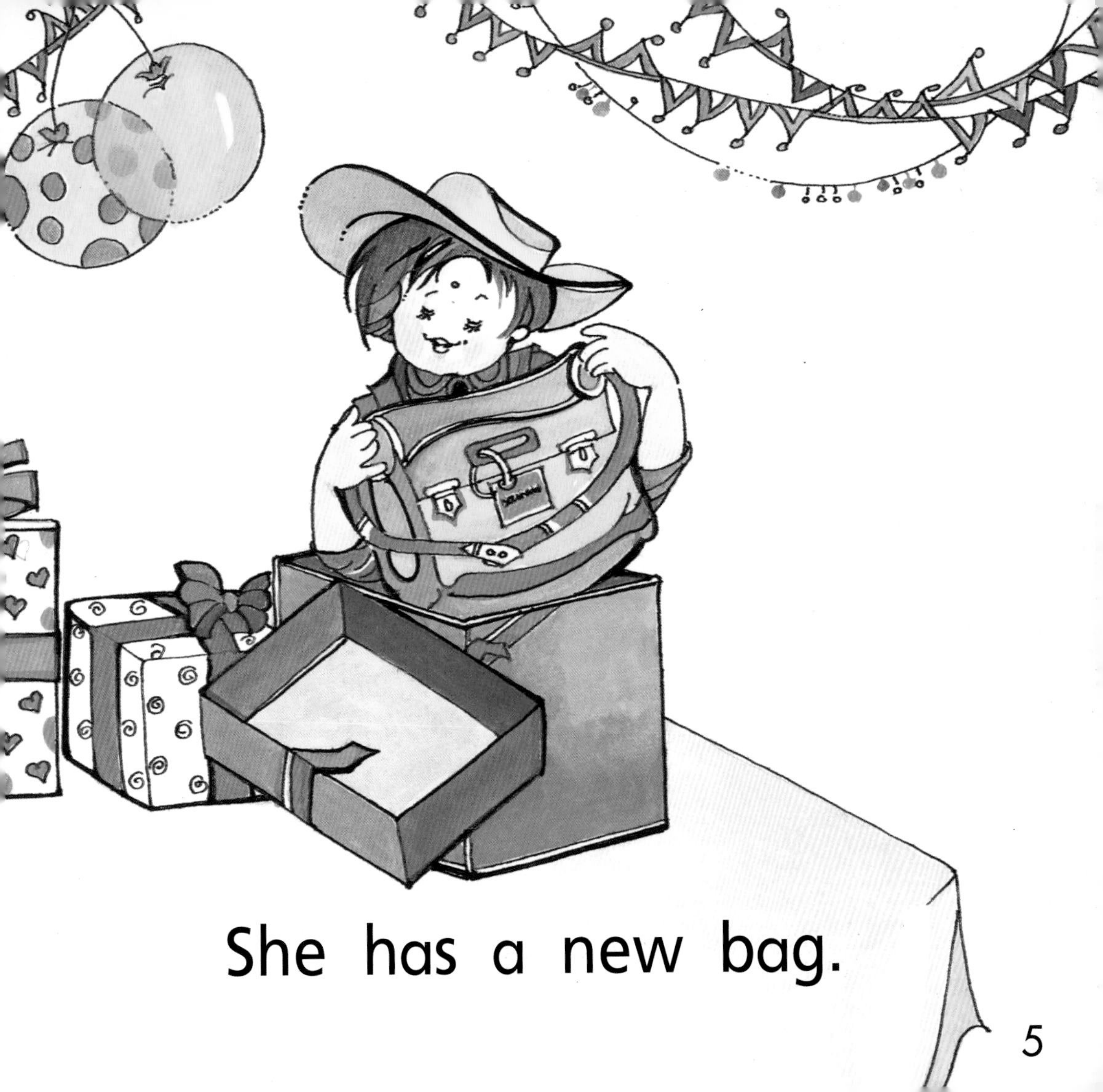

She has a new bag.

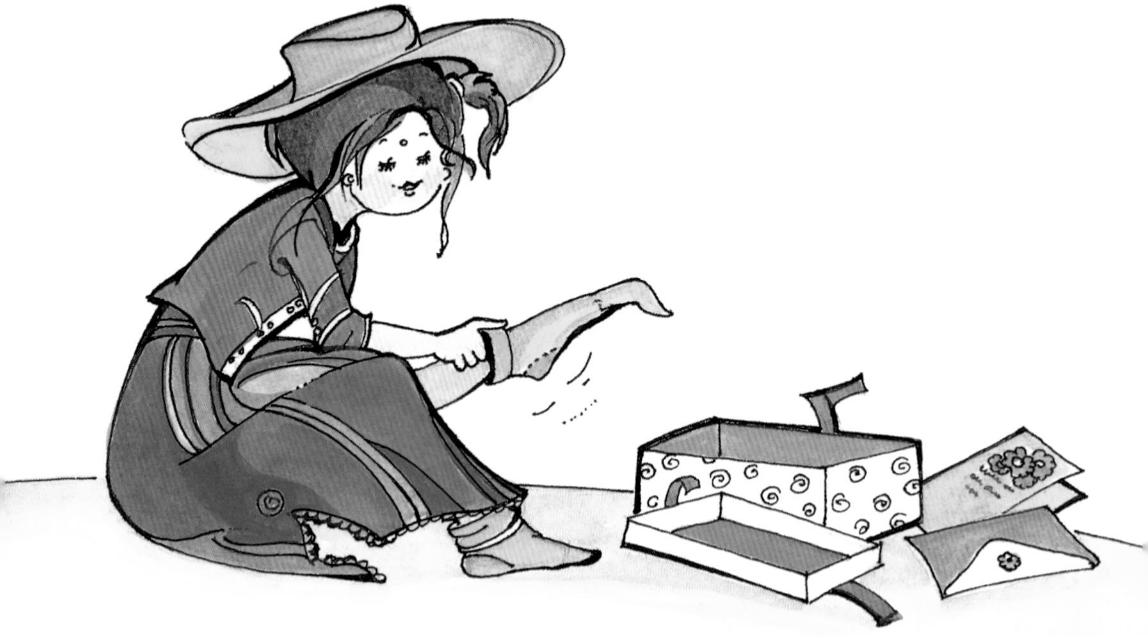

Neena has
some new socks.

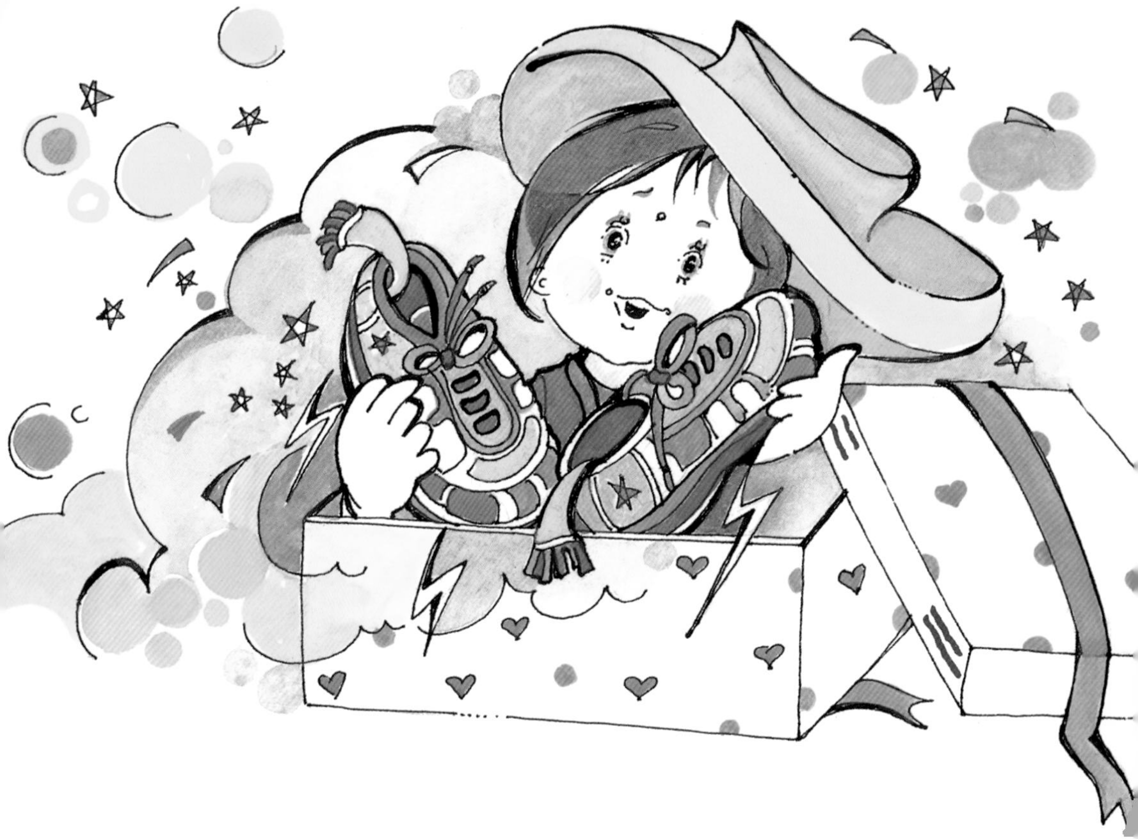

She has some new
jumping shoes.

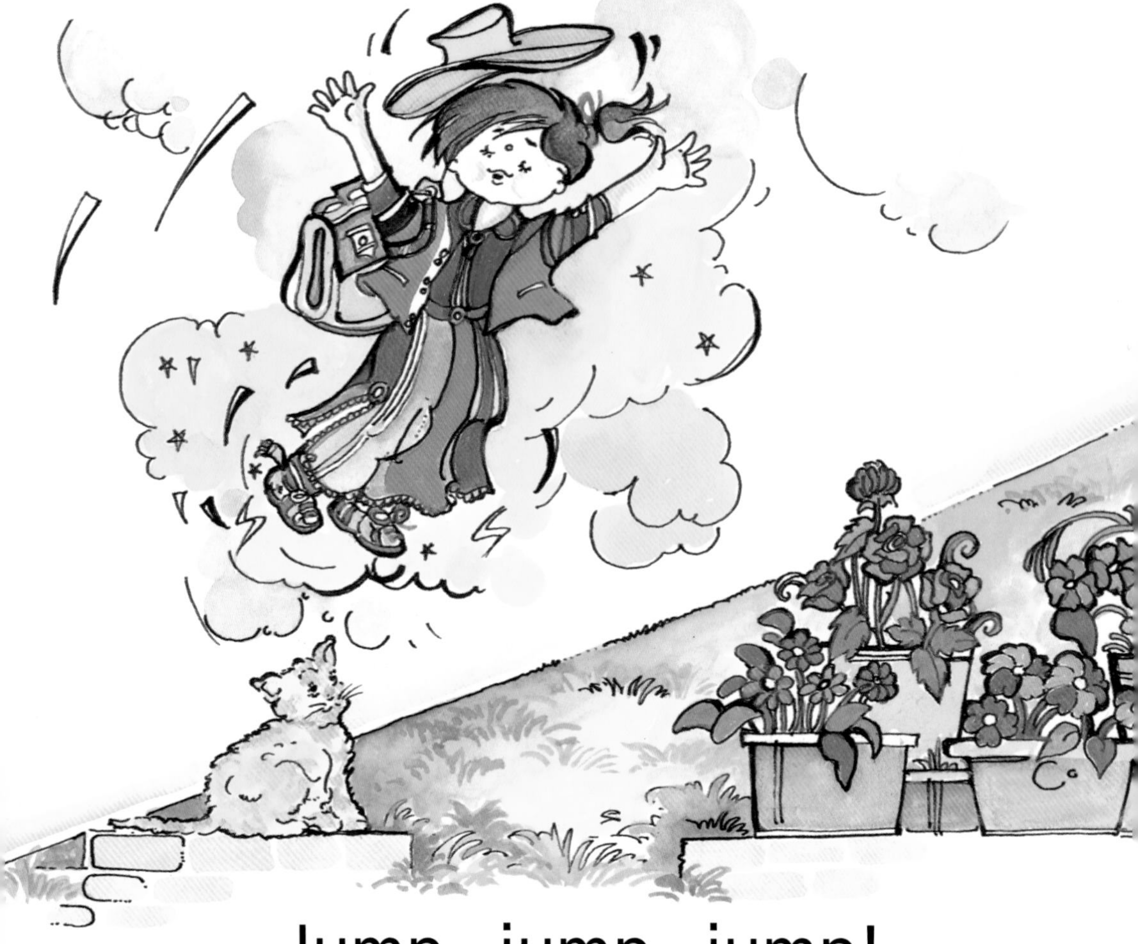

Jump, jump, jump!